N I G H T

H O M E

R O S E   T I T U S

Night Home

ISBN-10: 0990743357
ISBN-13: 978-0-9907433-5-4

Bathory Gate Press
P.O. Box 1916
Granbury, Texas

Visit our website at www.BathoryGatePress.com

BATHORY GATE
PRESS

NIGHT HOME

a Novella

Rose Titus

Her car pulled up into the driveway and she finally saw the house. She knew it from old photographs, but this was the first time actually seeing it. It wasn't huge for a Victorian era home, but it was big enough. The exterior was painted light gray, slightly faded from time, as if the old home had somehow managed to keep its dignity over the decades. She was the "last surviving heir" of a family almost died out, or so she was told. And the Victorian was all hers now, even though she hardly ever heard much about the eccentric granduncle who originally owned the place back in the 1930's.

She had no idea what to do with the place, or even if she could afford to keep it, repair it, or even pay the electric bills. She wondered if the electricity and plumbing were even functional, although she had been told that things would be in working order. *Oh, well, here it is.* She sighed. It was a long drive and she hoped it was civilized enough inside that she wouldn't need to go back up the highway to find a motel to stay in as night approached.

When she got in she found to her relief that the electricity did work, and so did the plumbing. The place was dusty, and needed a thorough cleaning. She had all of spring break from college to do that. And she needed to explore the place. What unusual things would she find lost or abandoned in the old Victorian?

She hoped the place wasn't haunted. There had been a murder nearby, she was told, way back in 1936. Her uncle, a professor, was killed, shot to death, by an associate from the university where he taught. The place had bad memories, or that's what she heard from elderly relatives who would say no more about it.

The place was lived in, from time to time. But it was so far from everything else that most people who lived there would later move on to be closer to the city. The last person to stay there was an elderly aunt that she hardly knew, and who had recently passed away.

It was all hers now. The only trouble was what was she going to do with it?

The first thing she did the next morning was shop for food. There was a small grocery store in the center of the rural town, along with a laundromat, a gas station, a coffee shop, a very small library, a thrift shop, a liquor store, a convenience store, and a pharmacy. Not much else. She wondered if the thrift shop was the most exciting place in town. No nightclubs, no major sized shopping mall... no... nothing. It was definitely what they meant when they described the place as "small-town America."

She came back to put the few grocery items away and noticed that the chrome-trimmed white refrigerator looked as though it came straight out of the 1950's. But it worked, even though its constant hum annoyed her. The oven, too, appeared to be a functional antique. The kitchen was lit with a fluorescent bulb, the kind her grandmother had in her kitchen back long ago. It flickered like a strobe light until it warmed up, causing ghostly shadows to appear in the dark corners. The toilets worked, but one of the sinks constantly dripped. The place needed updating badly. Either that or make a museum out of it. Then it dawned on her. There was no television.

"Where the hell is the—?" But then she realized that after Aunt Edna passed away there was talk about the place being broken into a few times. The window in the back door was smashed and had to be repaired soon. There was a piece of cardboard filling where the glass had been. That must have been how they got in. The television must have been taken.

"Whatever," she sighed, and wondered if the location was even too primitive to receive cable anyway.

Time to explore the place, and see if anything else was stolen.

She found silverware, genuine, she believed, not silverplate. It was beautiful, but needed to be cleaned and polished. She was glad it wasn't taken like the TV set. An old sable coat and hat in the closet upstairs. Old jewelry still tucked away in the bottom of drawers. It was like a treasure hunt. She wasn't sure if any of it would be worth anything, but she would eventually find out.

She continued to explore the rest of the ghostly old place.

In the basement there was nothing much but dusty old discarded furniture, a box of hand tools, piles of old books on science, abandoned and left stacked up on the cold stone floor. She noticed the books on science. They were dated from the 1920's and early 30's. Science then would be primitive now, she realized. But they were fascinating to look through. Most were on biology, botany, zoology. They must have belonged to the Professor, of course. The eccentric old granduncle. Most in the family simply referred to him as "The Professor." Professor Benjamin Aubrey — the man was nearly a legend in her family. A legend people seemed reluctant to talk about in much detail. Those in the family who knew of him said he had been working on something really unusual when he was killed. No one knew what it was, though. He was working on it, and kept to himself. He never spoke of his work. Then he was murdered. And no one talked about it much, as if there was a thick black wall of silence surrounding the past.

He was a distant relative, and it didn't matter now. But she was still curious.

There was a trap door for the ashes of the fireplace above, she noticed. It must be stuffed with crap, she thought. Out of boredom, she went to pull it open. She expected to be covered in soot, so she quickly stepped aside.

Nothing.

Nothing at all came out of the chute. She looked down to see if it was totally clean or if the ashes were instead grossly clumped together like a lump of black coal.

"What the—?"

Notebooks. A stack of them. "What the hell are these in here for?" She pulled them out. The yellowed pages were filled with handwriting. His strange project? It must be. Someone hid his notes in there. What a hell of a strange place to hide them. But why? So no one could steal his research? And what the hell was he working on? Maybe he was inventing something? Something that was commonplace today, like a microwave oven or a wireless phone?

She was alone in the house and had no television. What the hell, she thought, I might as well read over the old man's strange crap.

But first, she needed to go back up on the highway to find that pizza place she passed on the way last night. It was either that or Chinese. The idea of cooking on that antique stove didn't excite her much. And there was nothing else in town besides the lousy coffee shop, which she imagined to be run by waitresses with sixties hair and names like Lou Ann and Donna who called everyone "hon."

The first one began with, "I have made an astonishing discovery. The legends are true. "

What the hell is this stuff?

And she read on. He called his secret project his "Nocturnal Studies," and she wondered what on earth that could be about, and what the hell could he be studying in a quiet little town where nothing would ever happen anyway, especially at night?

Some of the notes were often more personal than scientific. All his academic life he had wanted to make a great discovery and finally he had found it — or it had found him. "The Nocturnal Race has made itself known to me after their search for a man of science with a suitably open mind..." Yeah, the Prof was known in the family history as being eccentric. But what had killed him? His discovery? And what was this Nocturnal Race he scribbled on about?

She sat in the out of date but functional kitchen and read on with the whir of the old refrigerator for background music until she noticed an old yellowed and faded news clipping dated September 7, 1936 tucked inside the notebook. *Professor Shot Dead.* "Oh my God." Her eyes scanned through the fragile paper. It was a colleague of his from the University who apparently suddenly went mad and shot him. The police hauled the murderer off after apprehending him at his office at the University. He was dragged away in shackles, raving about vampires.

What? The man who killed her granduncle was also wanted in connection with another murder.

And the Professor was studying the Nocturnal Race?

At least now she was sure his mysterious secret project didn't do him in. Instead, his death was caused by someone he unfortunately worked with at the university. But if the Professor was dead, then who hid the notebooks? And who put the clipping away in the book? Someone stuffed the notes safely away where no one could find them, and put away the clipping as if to preserve a tragic moment in time and hide the truth from the world. But who?

She would never be able to sleep now. She had all night to read. Could it be fiction, or even the writings of a brilliant man gone mad like his colleague? If it was, then why hide it away for years?Late into the night, her head was spinning with what she had read. It was after midnight and she couldn't stop reading the eccentric old man's notes. She remembered seeing a black and white photograph of him once, and so she could now imagine him scribbling into the notebooks with an ornate fountain pen. It turned out he bought the property just to study this "Nocturnal Race" he discovered.

"Oh God," she whispered. Why the hell didn't I stop at that liquor store? I sure do need it now.

They emigrated from Eastern Europe as a group in the 1850's to escape violent persecution, he wrote. A large spread of land was purchased for farming, sending people ahead of them to handle the purchase to make the transition more simple. They raised dairy cattle, sheep, goats, pigs...

She had noticed a few farms close by along the highway. The reading all seemed dull until she got to the part where they slaughtered the animals to sell the meat, and drank the blood themselves. They were in the habit of draining off small amounts from larger animals so they would not need to kill so many of them so often.

What?

Here it was written, as if a cold fact.

And the sun made them uncomfortable, so they stayed in during the day and slept, doing most of their work after dusk. Locals believed it was an odd foreign custom and therefore mostly caused them no trouble.

He wrote it as if it was all real. As if he truly believed in it himself.

Could it be? No... that would be just too crazy. She read on.

They were born that way, and certainly not dead or "undead." And had no supernatural abilities except that they were immune to most illnesses and often lived as long as three centuries... And they could see well in the dark.

Well, naturally.

What the hell am I thinking?

"This can't be real!" she muttered.

The rest of the notebooks seemed to contain information on various individuals with the "condition." She flipped through without reading in detail. There were names, ages—some as old as 150—occupations, comments on personality. "It just can't be real. I don't want to believe in this."

But on a deeper level, she did believe it. Somehow, she felt it was true.

She couldn't sleep at all now. It was one o'clock in the morning. She knew now that the entire night would be wasted reading this crazy stuff.

But the man died over it. So how could it be just nonsense? She needed to go outside, get some air and think. She needed to just get out of this old, creepy, poorly lit house. The refrigerator was still humming. She wanted to tell it to shut the hell up, but felt that if she did, it would mean that she was losing it.

"Shut the hell up!" It didn't work. The refrigerator still moaned.

She remembered there was an all-night convenience store off the highway, near the exit that led into the little town. It was well lit, and there would be other people in there, maybe. Maybe she would buy a few magazines, something else to read during her exile at the haunted mansion she'd been saddled with.

There was the usual convenience store stuff on the rack: Tabloids, celebrity gossip, fashion magazines, newspapers. The store sold lottery tickets, junk food, candy, beer, a few grocery items, even a few small appliances. She noticed the guy who owned the place was watching her. It made her nervous. Not because he watched her, but because he was so pale. He did not look unhealthy. It was like he just never got out into the sun.

"You must be the new girl."

"Huh?" She spun around to face him.

"You're new in town. You just moved into that old house."

"H-how do you know?"

"Well, how could I not know? I live across the field and saw the light was on for the first time in a long time."

"Oh," she felt silly. "Yeah. That's right. I'm new in town. The house will need some work, but it's not really that bad. My eccentric old uncle owned it a long time ago and —"

"I know. Professor Aubrey. He was a good man," there was sadness in his voice.

"Yeah, that's what they say —" how the hell would he know if he was a good man? This guy looked no more than thirty. The old guy had been dead for at least since 1936, according to the old newspaper clipping.

"Elton." He seemed to smile as he introduced himself. "Elton Masaryk."

"Muriel Aubrey."

"That's a pretty name."

She went up to pay for the magazine she picked.

"You let me know if you need anything over there, all right? I live just across the field. If you need anything, don't hesitate. Really."

"Thank you." She went for the door but turned around. "You sound as if you know something about Professor Aubrey?"

He hesitated. "A little. Why?"

"He was related to me, but I hardly know anything about him. I heard he was murdered by his colleague from the University and — "

"Yeah. That's right. The same guy who murdered your uncle also killed three other people too. They gave him the chair. Bastard deserved it." But then he was silent. He was beginning to sound as if he knew more than he could tell. As if it still angered him somehow. "Oh well." Then he went silent.

"Okay. Thank you." She left. She returned home as the sky began to brighten, and finally slept.

In the morning after getting very little sleep she had coffee and toast and sat with the notebooks at the table, reading them again. She promised herself she would put them all away, but she couldn't. She sipped her coffee and read the Professor's words. Were they the ravings of a madman? Or were they true? No. They couldn't be. It was impossible.

... They truly did have a reflection in a mirror. It was explained to the Professor that superstitious people believed that a mirror reflected one's soul, and also believed that the vampire had no soul, so therefore could have no reflection whatsoever.

Religious symbols had no effect.

The sun did not kill them outright. It slowly burnt whatever flesh was exposed. Heavy clothing gave some protection at times. But they preferred to sleep during the day... Well, of course, she thought. But she stopped herself again, reminding herself none of it was real.

"Intermarriage between the species is of course possible," one passage went on. "And it has occurred often enough throughout history for them to know that the child will most likely be like the father."

"What?" *This is not real. It's so not real. It's just not real...*

"Of course the wife is and always has been fully informed, although her family knows so little about the situation that they are more concerned for the fact that she is marrying a foreign immigrant from a land so far away they can hardly pronounce it or find it on a world map. She laughed and told me she found her father looking the country up in a book to find out where on earth it was."

Muriel recalled that one of the things she was told about her uncle was that he was the only professor at the University to advocate that women be one day admitted. He did get his wish many decades after his unfortunate death. On one occasion he was booed by an angry and shocked audience when he openly stood up to protest the University refusing to admit an African American student who had applied, but that was the way things were then. He almost lost his position, and was from then on continually passed over for promotion. Professor Aubrey was the type of man, she was told, who saw people as the same no matter who they were or where they were from. But back then, that just wasn't the way things were done.

"The difference in their culture has always been that women by necessity had to hunt alongside the men before domesticated animals became the main food source."

Hunting what?

"Centuries ago they went into the forests at night in small groups to hunt down deer or wild boar. Logically the women could not wait at home for the men to bring food home. A stag would be shot with an arrow, its throat cut as it fell dying. If anyone wanted to feed they needed to be present."

They hunted animals.

She was relieved.

Why should she be? *It wasn't real!*

"And so their women were almost never left at home with household drudgery. " He went on to describe their women as more physically fit than usual, "unlike our own women who become exhausted so easily."

Well, you would be too after cooking and cleaning and putting up with screaming brats all day, dear Uncle!

She read on... "The ancient people once worshipped them almost like gods before the coming of the Roman legions into their lands. Those primitives who worshipped the moon goddess believed they were her children, and sacrificed goats upon a stone altar to the goddess, draining the blood into a silver cup..." At that time, the Professor was told, the people lived side by side with the rest of humanity peacefully with no troubles. "It is only in recent centuries that they have been so persecuted and hunted."

It was all a great story. Too bad it wasn't real. She was almost beginning to believe...

She got the impression that the Professor felt them to be just like everyone else, except they slept all day. He seemed to respect their intelligence and character, even.

They lived what he referred to as "decent lives." This alone made her feel on edge, but she continued to remind herself it couldn't be real. What the hell made him write it? Stress?

Soon she noticed it was late afternoon and she was still in her pajamas. She had awakened very late in the morning, the old man's books making her become nocturnal herself. She tried to put them away but couldn't. She left them on the kitchen table and went to shower in the antiquated bathroom, where things still somehow seemed to work okay.

She was hungry again when she came out. She dressed and then went down and brewed another pot of coffee and began making a sandwich. She read some more...

After a while she noticed it was dusk and the sky was beginning to darken. Had she been reading the crazy old man's notes for that long all day?

There was a knock at the door, and she realized the doorbell of course no longer functioned. But who could it be?

"What? Elton? Hi. I didn't—" He was carrying a cardboard box.

"Hi yourself. The word around the neighborhood, if you can call this rural location a neighborhood, is that the place got broken into and the TV stolen, and so—" He came in and put the box on the table. "This is your welcome to the falling down old house present, from your neighbors across the field."

"Oh, no. You didn't have to. Look, that's expensive. Most people just bring over a pie." But she rushed to open the box. It was a small battery powered TV and she was overjoyed to see it. "Elton, thank you. Look, come in the kitchen. I'll get you some coffee, okay?"

"My store had an overstock. And no. I really don't need anything right now." But he followed her.

"Want a sandwich or—"

He stopped suddenly. "You found them? My God, you—"

"Found what?" Then she saw he was staring at the notes spread all over the table. "Oh. He was writing these papers. I —" She couldn't describe it. She didn't want to admit the old man was nuts.

"Where on earth did you find them?"

"Well, they were kind of in the basement, in this really weird place. You know the thing that you clean the ashes out of a fireplace with —"

"I think you mean a cleanout door —? They were in there?" He picked one up and began reading. "Muriel. People have been looking for these for a very long time. I don't know how to explain, but... these are so very important."

"Well, what do you mean? Either he wrote that stuff because he was losing it, or maybe he was under pressure from work. I don't know why he wrote it. You wouldn't believe some of the stuff in there."

"Muriel." He hesitated. "I know people who would be really interested in seeing these notebooks —"

"I... I think he died right after writing these."

"I know. It was... tragic. Well, I shall leave you alone to enjoy your new TV then."

"Elton, thanks. It was really nice of you. I should meet other people who live around here. You have family, right?"

"Yes. We live way across the meadow, just beyond the trees. That's how we knew someone was home. We saw a light on. Come visit some night when you have nothing else to do."

"Thanks. Sure you don't want coffee?"

"No. Thank you, though." He turned to leave.

"Hey!"

"*Yes?*"

"Elton? Who would want these ridiculous old notes?"

"Well, maybe it would be a conversation better saved for later. Hang on to them, okay? Don't... please don't throw them away. Maybe you shouldn't show them to anyone else, for now. All right?" He left.

The next morning she woke late again, but after breakfast she went to the local bakery and purchased a blueberry pie. On returning home she walked across the field with it towards Elton's house. She rang the bell, and there was no answer. She looked up and noticed the shades were pulled down in most of the windows upstairs. No one home, but why bother to pull down all the shades? Oh, well. She would try again later.

Later that evening, after running around the old place with a broom, she picked up the notes again. They had become irresistible now, even making her forget the new television set. What if it was all true? No, she reminded herself again. *It just can't be...*

She startled when there was a knock at the door. She looked out through the window and saw that it was Elton, and he was with someone this time. She went to let them in. "Hi, Elton."

"Muriel, hi." For a moment he hesitated. "This is another neighbor of yours. He lives down the road a bit, in an old farmhouse, almost as run down as yours—"

"Hi," she said enthusiastically, noticing Elton's friend was nearly as pale as he was, as if no one she had met in town so far ever went out in the sun. "I brought over a pie and knocked on your door, but—"

"Sorry," was all he said. Then he went silent. Suddenly, she noticed the tension.

But then the other man offered his hand. "Seymour."

She took it carefully.

"Seymour Zworykin." He smiled, almost warmly.

"Does everyone in town have a last name I can't pronounce?"

"The family that runs the gas station has the last name Jones," said Elton.

She laughed quietly. "Well, it's nice to meet you, Seymour. And it's nice to see you again, Elton. Let me get that pie—"

"Well... No. That's okay, Muriel," Elton continued. "No thank you. We're fine. Thanks."

"Won't you two at least sit down?"

So they did, both of them staring at the notebooks.

"Look, I am sorry about the mess on the table. I know they're dusty, and smell a little bad from being in the basement for like seventy something years. I know it's stupid, but I can't stop reading them. He wrote such off-the-wall stuff. You gotta at least let me get you coffee." She went to get two mugs.

"Miss Aubrey," Seymour began, "About the notebooks —"

"Why are you two so mysterious about those silly papers of his? And why don't you eat any of this nice pie I bought today? What is so —" Then it hit her. *"Oh my God."* She almost laughed, but stopped. And took a step back away from them both. "None of that stuff can be true. *Can it?"*

"Muriel —" Elton tried again. "Please. There is nothing to be afraid of. Look, your granduncle was a good man. He understood. We hope you will, too."

"I did not even freakin' know my uncle! *And will you two just tell me what the hell is going on? Because if you don't, I am so gonna scream —* "

It seemed to her like they had been talking for hours, and she had lost track of time when she calmed down. She realized also that she had finally stopped shaking. They were now in the living room. She had eaten both pieces of pie that were intended for Elton and Seymour, along with several cups of coffee, and she sat on the worn-out couch, listening to Elton talk, and taking it all in.

"It happened a long time ago, but it's still clear in my mind. I was just a boy then. I saw him come into the house with a gun so I hid in the closet... Then there was this awful hammering sound and I heard my father screaming... he had been asleep and then... I'll never forget that ungodly sound. I heard my mother scream. She tried to stop him. But it was no use. There was a gunshot. I heard her fall, and she stopped screaming. My mother was pregnant. I'll never know if I lost a brother, or a sister. Then I heard someone come in downstairs and two men arguing. It was Professor Aubrey. He had come to try and reason with him, but it was too late. I heard him shout, 'You have gone completely mad.' 'No,' said the other voice, much louder, 'It is you who have gone mad. These creatures are not human. They should all be destroyed. They are not like us,' and then he killed him as well. I remained hidden for quite a long time in that closet. It took a while for the police to arrive. Not everyone back then had a telephone, but someone did. I still to this day don't know who heard all the noise and reported it."

"But... that was a long time ago. You couldn't have been a little kid then. You'd be like—"

"Yes, I know. I don't look it."

"Oh... that's right. You guys... don't get old."

"Eventually," said Seymour. "We all have to go sometime. We just live a lot longer than most people. Miss Aubrey, we're sorry to have frightened you."

"No. Look, call me Muriel. I—you didn't scare me," she lied. "I was just... surprised that it was real, that's all. I didn't expect... well, you know..."

"Of course. We understand."

"Look, you want to take the notebooks, fine. Can't I just finish reading them?"

"Of course you can, Muriel," Seymour said. "It's not that we want them. You see, we just don't want them to get into the wrong hands. Four people already died because of superstition and ignorance. We don't want it to happen again. It's not just the two of us we need to protect. It's the entire community that could be put in danger. We have families, people we care about. Plus, we have to think of the well-being of the entire town. There are a lot of decent people locally who know about us but don't say anything. We have friends. They don't deserve people coming here from outside, knocking on doors, bothering people, asking questions. We don't want tabloid reporters and self-styled vampire hunters descending on us all, causing chaos, and maybe even hurting more innocent people... "

They talked of many things throughout the night, and it was nearly dawn when they left. She sat awake in bed staring out the window, watching the sun awaken into the sky and hearing the birds sing outside, knowing others were quietly sleeping. And she knew they would be safe.

She sighed before closing her eyes and imagined to herself that the notes would make a great story, and most would believe them to be fiction anyway.

And as she finally fell asleep, an idea awakened within her. *It would make a hell of a great story...* And before finally drifting down into oblivion, she decided she should wait until the right moment, and then ask if it would be okay.

"So...what do you all think?" She tried to sound cheerful, and hopeful. "I'll change all the names, the name of the town, the dates, and everything"

"Well," Seymour hesitated, and then he flatly said, "*No!*"

"Oh, come on, Seymour, she said she'd change everything necessary. It would be presented as pure fiction. You don't expect any modern person to believe—"

"No. No. And no! Bad idea. Very bad idea, Elton. Extremely bad idea."

"I think it's a good idea," said the attractive Sophie, whom Muriel just met that very evening. She wasn't expecting to meet any more of them so soon. Elton and Seymour had brought her over to introduce her to the Professor's niece. Sophie, she guessed, could be the oldest, but looked to be about 40. She might be the oldest, Muriel supposed, since she briefly mentioned in conversation how difficult things were for them in the old country. She seemed at times to have a slight accent, but it was obvious that she had been speaking English for a very long time. The others were quiet when she spoke. "Why not? Or did they all die for nothing?"

"No, Sophie, please. *It's not safe –* "

"Things change, Seymour. People change. Even the world changes."

"There are still fanatics running around in the daylight, you know."

"Well, if she changes names, they won't know where to run to. Will they?" And she turned to Muriel. "Let's rewrite your uncle's notes, then, dear. People will believe it's just a story." She then gave an almost sad look back at Seymour, "They put such awful things about us on television. Why not let someone write something different about us, for a change? A story that would be kinder to us? To change people's bad ideas about us? Aren't we all so tired of seeing such bad things about us, in books and in movies?"

Summer came while she busied herself with the seemingly endless cleanup and exploration of the old home, and summer then turned into autumn, and the autumn turned into winter. With the work about the house, the last remaining confusing paperwork for the estate, and getting settled in, it seemed as if she almost didn't notice the change of the seasons. She was now back at college; and her life started to get back into quiet and dull routine while spending weekends and winter break at the old house in the tiny little town. She got to know many people there, some who even knew her granduncle from long ago.

But she especially liked the company of Josephine, Seymour's granddaughter, who was closer to Muriel's own age. "They don't consider you a grown up around here until you're like 100 or something." Josie was still able to eat solid food, although bright light was beginning to make her uncomfortable. She was attending college, taking night classes. "Like the other day I was chewing gum and accidentally bit my lip. Ouch! Major safety hazard." Josie joked about it to cope. Her body was changing over as she grew into adulthood. She had stopped aging and had trouble staying awake during the day. Muriel learned a lot from Josie, who talked more freely, never having suffered any direct persecution herself.

Finally, word came one day that her story of "Professor Alberts" and the mysterious research that led to his tragic death would be serialized in her college's monthly publication. She would get no money for it, but she did get a free subscription; and it generated conversation among some of her classmates and friends. Only one thing remained the same, for she had changed the time frame to the 1950's, the location from New York State to Maine, the immigrants were from Romania instead of Czechoslovakia... she signed her own name to the story, written by Muriel Aubrey. Her friends were shocked. "Where did you get such a wild idea, girl?" "I dunno," she shrugged. "Too many late nights studying, I guess. Maybe too many beers." She couldn't wait to drive back to the rural town to share her news.

Sophie was especially thrilled for her, and she told her so. Sophie's real name, she learned, was Annasophia. It had been her idea to lead the entire group to America to save them from the constant persecution they had all suffered. "Wherever we went in the old country, there was trouble. The peasants were completely uneducated and ignorant. Maybe someday—Someday I hope things will change," she sighed. "We live in the dark, but why must we hide in it?"

"I'm sorry about how things were for you back then, Sophie," Muriel said, somehow knowing it hurt today as much as it did a century and a half ago.

"And now look at all the garbage you see on TV. The movies have us all as undead monsters," but then Sophie changed the subject to stop herself from becoming distraught. "How is school?"

"Pretty dull. I wish I could spend all my time out here in the boondocks."

And so she did. She decided to spend winter break with her new found family. That's what they all became to her. The small town did not have much to offer, but she spent as much time as she could there now. She often stayed awake late at night, with her uncle's old friends, and when she was with them she would sit by the fire at Annasophia's old stone house in the pine forest and listen to stories of the old country. Sophie told of how she believed there were no more vampires in Romania, because, she said, "they must all have been hunted to extinction by now." But the others would disagree and debate whether they were still there, surviving in small numbers somehow.

Muriel listened quietly one night while Sophie told of how she came home from a journey away from her small village to find her family butchered. "They died in their sleep," she whispered. But Muriel realized that they would have awakened to the terrible pain and shock of having a wooden stake pounded into them. It was then that Sophie, though still young, had to take leadership of a small group of survivors. She began, she said, by buying books to teach herself and the others English, "and I read as much as I could about America, and made plans for what was left of us to come here to start over."

During the darkest, cold winter nights, they discussed anything and everything — the past, the present, the future... art, science, philosophy, and even what was on television. Muriel would sit by the hearth and listen but eventually she would get tired and go home.

One morning she woke up with the wind howling and snow flying outside her window. She looked sleepily outside to see a field of endless white that ended at the edge of the forest. She yawned, looked down, then startled. "What?" she said out loud. There was a man, standing there, at the edge of the trees, looking up at the old house, oblivious that she could see him. He wore a down parka, ski hat, and those ugly hiking boots that a lot of men wore out in the snow. "Who the hell... ?" She wished Elton was awake so she could call and ask 'do you know that guy?'

What the hell is he doing in my woods?

But then silently he turned and walked away. Like an apparition, he was gone. She put on her coat and boots to look in the snow and there she saw footprints. He was real, not imaginary. Then who in the hell was he? She knew it wasn't anyone who once knew her old long gone granduncle. The sun wasn't out, but still it was day. She ran quickly back in, shivering from the ice cold wind.

Late in the afternoon, she called Josephine, who woke earlier than the others.

"Huh? Some weird guy in your backyard? Call the cops."

"He's gone now, Josie." There was no sign of him now.

"Got a strange boyfriend stalking you or something?"

"No way. Don't know this guy. Hell, couldn't even make out his face with the snow flying around, but I kind of think he was maybe middle-aged, the way he walked and stuff like that."

"I still think you should call the cops."

"Naw. They'll think I'm nuts."

Later, Seymour and Josephine came over to see if she was all right. "Of course I'm okay. It was just some fruitcake lost in the woods, that's all."

"In a blizzard? What kind of fool goes out in the kind of storms we have around here?" Seymour said.

"Let's go look through the woods," Josie suggested.

"You want to search the woods in sub-zero temperatures?" Muriel couldn't believe she would even want to. "It's freezing cold in the daytime, and it must be even colder now."

But they went back out. Muriel stayed in, watching her new television that lacked cable. Soon, they were back at the door.

"No sign of anything," Seymour said. "But there probably wouldn't be because of the snow fall earlier. No one is out there now, Muriel. You're safe."

"Look, I'm not worried. I'll lock my door. You guys are making more of this than I am."

"Can't be too careful these days. If you see anything again, call someone."

They left. She decided to forget about it and go to bed. And to try not to feel ridiculous.

The next morning she decided laundry needed to be done. She had no clean underwear left, or clean socks, and she wanted to wash the sheets and bedspread she had brought with her from the dorm, as they still smelled like her roommate's constant smoking, another reason she was glad to move into the run-down old house. The blizzard was finally all cleared out and the sun shone brightly, reflecting in the pure white snow that now covered the rural landscape. She looked out into the forest behind the house; she could only see the trees, all covered in white. At night the moon would come out and they would all turn silver.

After locating a snow shovel and clearing a path for her car, she gathered her things and headed into town to the laundromat. The heater in her car was ineffective, and the heat in the laundromat wasn't much better. When all sorting and folding was done, she decided to head for the local coffee shop, which, she guessed, was probably the most exciting place in a town with no cable, a one room library, a liquor store, a thrift shop, and a single gas station.

Perfect place for a bunch of vampires, she thought to herself. No one around to bother them. And she wondered how many other people locally, if any, knew.

"No one around to bother them," she whispered, loading the trunk of her Chevy with clean smelling laundry. And she realized, that's why they stay here.

The coffee shop was populated by what she felt were stereotypical small town type folk, she noticed. Old people reading the paper, having breakfast, and complaining while they read about this politician and that politician and complaining about the general way things were today... She ordered a coffee and donut.

Further down along the counter sat a man who didn't look local, and he appeared vaguely familiar somehow... He also ordered coffee, and a bagel, and, "By the way, since you most likely live around this area, I'm traveling through and looking for a house that once belonged to a man who's last name was Aubrey?"

She startled, and looked at him. Had it been him in the woods?

"Nope, don't know anyone by that name 'round here," said the waitress with the out-of-style blonde perm.

And Muriel was relieved.

"How about you, miss?" he said, looking directly at her.

"N-no... sorry. Can't tell you." She sipped her coffee and remained silent. She watched him warily from the corner of her eye for nearly a half hour until he finally finished his coffee and left.

And when he walked out the door she was sure. It was him.

"We respect people's privacy around here."

"Huh?" She startled again, and then had no idea how to answer.

The waitress said nothing else, and turned her back to Muriel. She quietly went back to her work, wiping counters, brewing more coffee.

Muriel was secretly grateful. And she felt foolish for previously snickering quietly to herself at the middle-aged waitresses, who most likely spent their whole lives working in a cheap, boring diner in a small town. She realized these women could probably know a hell of a lot from living and working and listening in a place like this, and most likely knew a lot more than they were saying. What, and how much, was the question.

When she returned home, she recognized Josie's small gray Saturn by the side of the road next to her driveway, waiting for her return. She got out of her Chevy and simultaneously Josie got out of her car. "What's up, Jos?"

"I was worried, that's what's up. Someone we know called, said some strange guy is wandering around town, asking all kinds of questions."

"Yeah. It's true. I ran into him today." She went to get her laundry out of her car. "Let's get inside. It's colder than hell out here."

Once inside, Muriel put the tea kettle on and explained.

"Muriel, I'm worried. That is so strange. A guy is wandering around in your woods, staring through your window, and going around town asking about stuff."

"I dunno. It's getting damn spooky. I mean... " her voice trailed off when she realized the irony. She was surrounded by vampires all around town, and she was suddenly terrified by an odd, middle-aged, out-of-shape man in a donut shop. "It's just not... logical."

Josephine declined to have tea or cookies. She just couldn't stomach it anymore, she said. Muriel felt bad for her, unable to imagine a life of not being able to eat whatever she wanted. They sat and talked awhile.

"The way he sounded, he seemed educated. He was middle-aged, or older. But not old. I dunno. Hard to tell. He didn't seem strange when I saw him at the coffee shop, but being in my woods is strange. And asking questions about my uncle is very damn strange. Who would even remember him? Except you guys—"

"What was that?"

"What was what?"

"Muriel. I heard something."

"Oh, come on. You're just getting paranoid like me." She could hear nothing at all.

"No... I... It sounds like a car out there."

She looked through the window, and then finally Muriel noticed. "Who the hell is that?"

Josie got up to look out the front window too. "I don't think I recognize that truck, Muriel."

"Oh God —"

"He's leaving now, though. Whoever it was, it was like he was parked there on the side of the road by the house, and now he's gone."

"I am scared, Josie. I don't know what to do."

"Maybe you should move back on campus."

"No. What's that gonna solve? Then you'd all still be in trouble, and it would be my fault. I... I can't just walk out like that."

"You're a good person, just like your uncle," she was still staring out the window. Her voice was distant and sad. "I never knew him, but I wish I did. People who can accept us are so few and rare. There are so few people we can tell, except for around this little town. A lot of people grew up here, don't see us age, know the old stories, and know enough not to hurt us. And it's not your fault. No one will blame you." She turned to look directly at Muriel. "And, Muriel... I'm afraid, too."

"I don't know what to do." Muriel sat down on the worn out sofa, and gazed out the window into the cold darkness.

"Maybe we should tell Sophie. She already knows about this guy, but tell her about that strange vehicle too."

Muriel agreed. They would tell her right away, as soon as it was dusk.

"... So this guy I'm seeing, right? He's local, but there are some things I gotta tell him because I think he wants to get serious." She took a left turn. "I mean, we do things a little differently, and I'm afraid that would freak him out. He knows some things, but not everything."

"What's to freak out about? He'd only lose a few drops," at least that's the way she understood it to be, from her uncle's notes. "Right?"

"Well... you know how they show it on TV. You see somebody get their throat ripped to shreds then they die two seconds later. I wish TV was never invented, Muriel. You know that?"

"Yeah, I know. But I sure missed not having one until now."

"Here we are," Josie pulled up into the driveway of the small stone house that was partially hidden behind a row of pine trees, making Sophie's house difficult to see from the road. Annasophia opened the door. "What is it, my darlings?" she asked in a motherly tone. "Come in, then. Come in, children."

Muriel did not think of herself as a child. But then Sophie was so much older...

"Sophie," Josie began, "We wanted to tell you, someone is watching Muriel's house."

"Yeah. Some strange SUV was out on the road, looking in the window."

They followed her inside. Sophie was speechless at first. She brought them into the living room, where she had her sewing machine out. She had been making a dress. She owned a seamstress shop with another woman in town, and took work home with her often. Muriel heard that customers came from many other surrounding towns to find her shop, because her work was so high quality.

She put her fabric away and sat down. "This is my fault. I let this happen."

"No," said Josie. "Sophie! How can it be your fault?"

"Yeah, if it's anyone's fault, it's mine," said Muriel. "Right?"

"No, not right. It's my responsibility, if anything happens." She looked as if she was in pain. "Dear God. I don't want this to ever happen again."

"It's not your fault, Sophie. I'm sorry I ever sent that story to that magazine. I should have kept quiet about it. I was a jerk to—"

"No, Muriel. Sit down, both of you. Let me tell you something. Muriel, I must ask you. How many of those old notebooks did you find?"

The girls sat across from her. "Five," Muriel said. "Why?"

"Well. That's what I thought you had, that night when I saw them on your kitchen table. But... I remembered that he had six of them. You never found any other notebook?"

"N-no."

She sighed. "That has me worried. You see, the way I remember — and it's been such a long time — He was planning to show some of his notes to another professor at the university. I asked him not to, and I thought that he wouldn't, but... I saw them in his car and asked where he was going with them. He told me. I begged him not to. He agreed, then, not to show his research yet. But he left them in his car. Then he claimed one of the notebooks had disappeared. I was worried then, and he never found it. We all looked everywhere. Shortly after, he and the others were murdered. In a panic, I quickly gathered up all his papers, everything I could find that he had kept, and hid them as well as I could. I was in a hurry, and put them there because it was the only available hiding place at the time. And who would bother to look in there? No one that I know cleans that thing out."

"You put them in there? In that... " She couldn't think of the exact name for it. "That place?"

"Yes." She looked down at the carpet, drew a breath and let it out slowly. "I put them in there quickly the night after the murder, before the police came to search the house. I always planned to one night somehow get them back and, I don't know, just put them someplace else. But then people moved in. They never found them, thankfully. It was just lucky they never used the fireplace much, I suppose. But then most people are too lazy to bother to clean their ashes out... "

"Um... Sophie? Was it you who broke the window in the back door? I mean, maybe, trying to get them back, or something?"

"No. That was most likely just stupid teenagers stealing the TV to sell for drug money. Anyway, we knew the Professor had a spare key somewhere in the garden and I was looking all around for that, too, but never found it."

"Oh. Sorry I thought—"

"Never mind. What I need to tell you is... I think it may be my fault your uncle was killed. "

"*What?*"

"Well, I had followed his story in the newspaper for some time, about how he got in trouble at the university for advocating for blacks and women to be admitted. He seemed so far ahead of his time. In the old country, they always treated us like... well, worse than animals when they found out about us. Killed us outright with no good reason. It was like how the people in the South treated the blacks, you know... Back then, that's how things were, and I saw it being similar somehow." She paused, sighed again. "I heard he was coming to our little town to research the local legends for his folklore studies. Yes, dear Muriel, the little town has legends of vampires the way Salem, Massachusetts has legends of witches. At the time he arrived, we had been here long enough for the less educated people to whisper. That was in the 1930's, and that foolish Dracula film had been in the theaters. It caused some talk. He came here to do research. I went to the house he was renting at the time, which he eventually purchased to stay long term. I went to introduce myself and, well, you girls know the rest. If I had kept quiet, he would have believed there was nothing here but foolish stories and he would have written his paper and then he would have gone home. But no. I had to believe that I could change things, make things better for us all. I was wrong. It was my fault, and it still is."

"*No!*" Josephine stood up. "No! No! *And no!* It is not your fault. Okay? You did not pull the trigger, Sophie. That guy did, whoever he was. And he went to jail for it. And then he got the chair, okay? It is not your fault—"

"Sophie," Muriel broke in. "You haven't been carrying all this guilt around for like eighty years?"

"Well... Yes."

"Well, don't, because it's not your fault. If it's anyone's fault, it's the guy who pulled the trigger, like Josie said. Plus also, it's my uncle's fault. Because he talked to someone about it. And maybe he was stupid enough to take the notebook back to the university with him, and lose it, or let someone see it, or whatever. But that was his mistake, not yours."

"No one blames you, Sophie," Josie went to her and put her arms around her. "We love you."

"Yeah, we love you, Sophie," and Muriel put her arms around her, too.

"Thank you. You girls are wonderful. Well...that's not everything, Muriel."

"Then what...?"

"Before he was shot, Benjamin said he believed that some of the notes might have been stolen from out of his car, by the other professor, the very same man who committed the murders, when my dear Ben refused to let him see them. That was right before he was killed, of course."

"But that guy is dead now," said Josie. "They gave him the chair."

"I know. Then who is this who keeps watching us? And what ever happened to the missing notebook? Could someone else have found it, and read it?"

They talked about it for hours but could come to no conclusion. Sophie invited Muriel to stay the night, saying she would be safer than alone. But Muriel felt more comfortable in her own bed, and besides, she said, "I'd feel stupid being scared over this."

"Worse things have happened than strange cars out on the street." Sophie picked her stitching back up. "Well...be careful then. Lock your doors!"

Josie drove her home.

"So, what's this guy's name?"

"Huh?"

"The guy you're interested in?"

"Oh. Joel. He's cool. His dad is a truck driver who doesn't know anything about me, which is probably good. I mean, he knows I'm seeing Joel, but he doesn't, you know, *know* about me. He doesn't know what he wants to do with his life. And I still haven't figured out if I'm interested in him or not."

"Yeah. Whatever." She hesitated. "Josie. I was wondering... how do they get the blood out of the animals? I mean, in the notes that I saw he didn't say — "

"They just use a needle. I've seen it done. It doesn't seem to hurt them. They just stand there, the big stupid 800 pound dairy cows. What? You thought we bite them? With all that smelly fur?"

"Nope. I didn't think that. That would be like the old-fashioned way, I guess. I thought maybe a knife, or something, and then have to stitch them up." She did at least know it was bottled and refrigerated, and she had seen it put in a microwave.

"Naw. That would be a mess." She explained there were two large farms outside of town, with about five hundred cattle in total, more than enough to feed forty nine of them.

"There are that many?"

"I dunno, four or five hundred dairy cows —"

"No! I mean —"

"Oh yeah. You only met a few of us. Yeah. The population hasn't gone up much since the 1800's, I guess." She explained that they had fewer children than most people, though they weren't certain why. It didn't matter, probably. "After all, we live longer anyway. I guess we don't need to replace ourselves as often. I ought to take biology in college. Maybe I can figure some of this stuff out."

She turned on the car's heater, but still they were both cold. It was always colder at night.

They talked about school. Josephine went nights; it was easier for her to stay awake if she did. She worked part-time also as a waitress at a truck stop. "Some of the men who come in there are such pigs. Last week one of them grabbed my ass."

Muriel laughed and said she was working her way through school until she found out she had an inheritance. "Enough to pay for school, fix the car, get a few new pairs of decent jeans, along with a big old house. Now I don't have to work until the money runs out, so no one grabs my ass. At least for now."

"You are so damn lucky, you know that. You get to go to school for free, girlfriend! And that pisses me off—" Josie began to look in the rearview mirror. "Hey. That car isn't following us? Is it?"

"I didn't notice anything," Muriel looked behind. "I... I dunno."

"Let's hope not. It does kind of look like the one that was parked on the street."

"Yeah. Let's hope not." She tried to put it out of her mind. "And don't be pissed off. I go to school for free, but you live longer and you'll never get fat!"

"Yeah? And now some creep is following both of us, and I don't think he wants to grab our ass!"

"So, step on it. Hit the gas, will you?"

"No. It will tip him off. Besides, it's icy. I'm driving to the police station."

"Does this town even have a police station?"

"Yeah, we've got three cops and a smelly hound dog, or something like that."

As usual, Sergeant Stepanek was working the night shift. It didn't seem as if anyone else was at the small police station. Josephine introduced Muriel quickly and told him what was going on. "Yeah. Muriel Aubrey. Nice to finally meet you. How do you like the old house?" He had a mug with a lid on his desk. Muriel guessed it wasn't coffee.

"It's a little drafty," she admitted, realizing that he and Josie knew each other, and then she wondered if the sergeant knew anything about the break in. "But most of the electrical things work okay, sort of, and it's cool to have my own house instead of being stuck in a dorm with this bunch of idiots partying all night while I'm trying to study."

"Good... well, anyway, " he went on, "Yeah, there has been some loser wandering around asking strange questions. We talked to him, asked if he was lost, can we help out, that sort of crap. He says he's doing a research paper on the incident, which happened back in '36 — I think that was the year? I'd leave it at that, for now. He seems harmless, so far. He's definitely not from around here. No one knows where he's staying, though. Probably one of those cheap fleabag motels up the highway, but that's just a guess. Or probably he commutes back and forth from wherever. I do know he's been checking public property records, which is very strange. And people have seen him driving around at night for no apparent reason. Someone at the library saw him photocopy pages out of a phone book, which is also strange. So this is some kind of research he's doing." He looked directly at Muriel now. "Hey, you know your place got broken into?"

"Yeah. Did you ever catch them?"

"Nope. Previous to having this strange guest, we thought it was kids because more than once we caught kids breaking in to that house to smoke dope and fool around with their girlfriends. I've had to chase them out a few times. But now we're not so sure this guy had nothing to do with it."

"He's been in my house?"

"No, we're not sure, remember? Don't worry about it, for now. We've got our eye on him. Okay? Keep safe, just watch your back. That goes for you too, Josie. And if he bothers either of you, you call me right away."

"T-thank you," said Muriel. "I'm glad you know about it, at least. By the way, we came because . . . we kind of thought someone might have followed us."

Sergeant Stepanek followed the girls back to Muriel's house in his squad car, and made a quick check around the area surrounding the house. "Looks clear, girls. Nothing out of the ordinary. Muriel, is your phone in good working order?"

"Yeah. I think so."

"Got a cell, too?"

"Yeah."

"Good. If you see him again, or if you think he's following you — "

"I'll call. Thank you, Sergeant. I appreciate it. Everyone I've met so far has been really good to me."

He left. The girls stood in the ice-covered driveway watching his car drift back down the darkened winter road.

"You gonna be okay?" Josie asked.

"Yeah, I think so," she gave the other girl a hug. "Okay. I'm finally gonna go to bed. Watch out for guys who wanna grab your ass."

They laughed.

"I'm glad I met you, Josie. All of you. But especially you."

"I am too. I wish I had known your uncle."

They said goodbye, and Josie drove away.

She woke up late the next day, and, looking out the window into the vast snow-covered emptiness, she half wondered if it had all been just a dream, not just the night before, but the past several months and all she had learned and everything she now knew.

But then she looked under the old brass bed and saw that the notebooks were still there, safe where she had left them. Yes, she sighed, it was real. And, unfortunately, so was her stalker, whoever the hell he was.

Muriel made coffee, showered, and dressed in last night's clothes that had been left on the floor next to her bed. She had nothing to do today except prepare for returning to college after winter break was over. It would be hard to return to her friends at college and not be able to talk about everything that was happening in her life. 'Muriel! What did you do on winter break? I went to Cancun!' 'Oh, hi Trudy! No. I didn't go anywhere special. I just hung out with a bunch of vampires and did my laundry, cleaned the house, and was chased by a maniac stalker, that's all.'

She went out to her mailbox, hoping last semester's grades had come in. She couldn't access them online, since the old house wasn't connected in any way, yet. She was also quietly hoping another check from the liquidation of the stocks held by the estate would arrive. She did plan to put some of the money away for the future, one of these days. It then dawned on her that eventually that unfortunate time would come when she would need to get an actual job and earn a living. The funds wouldn't last forever...

She pulled open the ice-covered mailbox. The grades did not arrive. No check for $57,895.83 either. That was the amount she was told over the phone by the lawyer's office. It would be the last in the series she was receiving after the liquidation of stock. A catalog of underwear did arrive, and another catalog of accessories, and a catalog from her college with class schedules. "What the hell is this?" There was an envelope with no stamp, no address. It just said "Miss Aubrey" on it.

"Oh, my God." She held it and her hand shook. She was afraid to open it and she already guessed from whom it might be from. She looked around and knew she was alone, nothing near but snow, ice, the frozen landscape, the cold pavement under her feet and the ancient drafty house up the driveway. She wished Elton, or Sophie, or Josie, or even that cynical Seymour could be standing next to her now while she opened it. But it was daylight, and she was alone.

Why the hell couldn't she find a vampire when she needed one?

Dear Miss Aubrey,

I apologize for not being able to introduce myself in person, but after having read your story, which you have recently published, I hope that you would agree to meet with me and discuss certain unusual events, which took place so many decades ago.

"Oh, dear God." She dropped the letter on the pavement and bent to pick it up out of the slush. There was no other way to contact this person other than with the cell phone number at the bottom of the page. It continued.

Of course, you must realize that your fictional story is remarkably similar to a true incident, which did occur, and therefore I would like to know what was the source of your inspiration? Although the events took place many decades before you were born, you seem well acquainted with previously unknown and well hidden details. For instance, the assertion of your "Professor Alberts" that vampires were and still are a "nocturnal race" or sub-species of mankind originating in Eastern Europe, is highly unusual...

"Shit," she hissed out loud in the frigid air. "He knows. This crazy whack job knows." And she knew what she had to do as soon as it was dusk. Show Sophie... and call the police sergeant who worked the lonely night shift. She cursed the day she re-typed her uncle's notes and hoped no one would be hurt this time around.

A fire lit the small living room in Sophie's old house, and there was little other light except for a small table lamp. That was one of the first things Muriel noticed, that they felt comfortable in the dark. She had almost gotten used to darkness herself from association. She listened as Sophie read the letter outloud to the small group.

"Well," Josie spoke first after Sophie put the letter down. "Maybe just try denying everything? I mean, no one believes in us now anyway."

"Josephine," Seymour sounded serious, as usual. "He obviously already believes. Accept the fact that we are now in a great amount of trouble—"

"*I'm sorry*," Muriel interrupted. "I shouldn't have done this. I just thought, well... if I wrote it, then maybe it would do some good, and some day people would be able to understand, and... maybe... make people know it's wrong how they've treated you for so long. I guess that's why I wanted to write it. *This is my fault* – "

"No, Muriel. No," Seymour held up a hand and spoke softly, his voice not so cold as it often was. "Look, we all agreed it would be all right for you to write it. You didn't just go ahead and do it yourself."

"Don't go and blame yourself, Muriel," said Elton. He sat across from Sophie, and was silent up until now. "You and Josie are just kids. You don't know how bad things can get. You haven't lived long enough to know how downright dangerous people can be. Then again, Josie might be right. You can deny it all, say you dreamed it up from hearing stories about your mad scientist uncle."

"Yeah, and I can't arrest this guy for writing a letter, either," Karl Stepanek pointed out, "Look, people," and he went out to the kitchen and helped himself to what was in the refrigerator. "He's been watching us; the people on the day shift have let me know, something is going on with this guy," and Muriel watched as he put a ceramic mug into the microwave. "How 'bout we do some of our own surveillance?"

"What? Get a video of this nut hanging outside my house watching me?"

"No," he came back into the living room and returned to the worn out couch. "Meet him. But don't be alone. We'll be watching. It's my bet he doesn't know what we look like. The idiot probably expects us to be wearing all black, for Christ's sake."

And that was the second thing she noticed when she first met them. They looked almost liked everyone else, and dressed like everyone else. And except for being pale, it would be difficult to tell them apart from most people.

"Find out what the hell the fool wants. Then we decide what to do about it."

"So what is your plan, Karl?" said Sophie. She picked up her sewing. "We are all listening."

The truck stop really was as busy as Josie said it would be, and noisy, too. She looked around and felt transported back in time to a fifties diner, and that was the look of the place. The crowd was composed of truckers, business travelers, and she imagined, a few lovers running away together... plus a few others only she knew about.

"Can I get you some coffee, hon?"

She looked up, surprised to see Josie in her waitress uniform, and reminded herself she wasn't supposed to know her. "Yeah. Please get me a large decaf, and a donut. Thank you, miss."

Josie stifled a giggle.

This jerk better show, she said to herself. He wanted to meet me, then this is it. Instead, he had tried to insist on a place more private. *Yeah, right. As if I would meet him somewhere alone.*

She gazed down at the menu before her, pretending to read it. She was worried, as she had been since that afternoon in the coffee shop when she first saw him. And she realized, for the first time in her young life, she was really, truly afraid. Not of what might happen to her, but of what might happen to other people she had learned to care about. Her parents passed away when she was little, and she hardly remembered them. All she knew was that her grandmother complained of 'damned drunk drivers,' which she came to realize was the cause. Now her grandmother was gone, and she had no one else besides herself.

"Miss Aubrey?"

She startled, awakened suddenly from her thoughts.

She looked up and saw her stalker. "Oh... ah... hi." It was all she could say.

"May I sit down?"

"Yeah. Okay."

The middle-aged man pulled out a chair and sat. "I was hoping that we could have met somewhere more quiet?"

"This place will do just fine. And I don't think I caught your name, since you signed your letter with your phone number?" Finally she got a better look at him. He was putting weight on a once trim frame and his graying hair seemed slightly unwashed. His clothes were clean, almost new, but not expensive. But the first thing she noticed was that he carried a worn out briefcase.

"Yes, of course. Sorry about that. Michelson. Darren Michelson. My grandfather was a colleague of Professor Aubrey."

"Huh? Oh. That's what you wanna talk about?"

"Partially, but that's not all. I apologize for the mysterious letter I left for you. You see, lately I had been surfing the internet for information on vampires, and saw mention of your story. After reading it, I then began asking around for you, and no one seemed to know much, which is unusual since it's a small town —"

"Well, I guess they don't mess in other people's business. But what about my uncle? He's been dead a long time. I have no idea what this is about."

"You are of course aware of what your uncle was researching?"

"So? Just a crazy eccentric relative of mine. That's all."

"But how do you feel about it? Do you believe that such things could exist?"

"Naw. That would be ridiculous. Just an old story told about the Professor."

Josephine came quietly by with Muriel's coffee. Darren ordered a black coffee for himself. "What if there was evidence?"

"What evidence? There is no evidence. Evidence of what?"

"Of the existence of actual vampires." He lowered his voice. "Which is exactly what your uncle was studying when he was killed—"

"Yeah? And was he by the way killed by your grandfather, Darren?"

"Yes." He hesitated. "And for that... I really am sorry. But that happened so very long ago, it's way beyond anyone's control. I'm sure you understand that, Miss Aubrey. People in my family all whispered about it. But there was evidence. And it was kept hidden, all these years. I used to continually wonder about it as a kid. Then I continued to wonder about it all for the rest of my adult life. I have a boring life, actually. I'm an accountant. Have two kids forever in college who keep changing their majors. House in the suburbs. Wife left me for someone else five years ago. Got laid off, re-hired, then laid off again. But none of that is unusual. That's all just life. But all my life, I've had this," he reached into his briefcase. "And kept on wondering about it."

There it was. The Sixth Notebook that everyone had been looking for since 1936. She suppressed her excitement and pretended to be annoyed. "So?"

"It's your granduncle's handwritten notes on the subject. I'm afraid to say it may have been stolen from him at the university, or obtained some other way by less than ethical means. Would you like to read some of it? He writes of actual nocturnal blood drinking beings, capable of living centuries. It's intriguing, almost frightening. Thinking of it kept me awake many nights. He was living in this very town, Muriel. Did he ever feel his life to be in danger? Do you?"

"Darren. His life was in danger. From his esteemed colleague."

"And once again, I am sorry. But do you believe it to be possible? I mean, think of the implications in this. Have you perhaps noticed anything unusual in this town?"

"Like what?" She sipped her coffee, trying to play disinterested.

"I don't know. Anything?"

"Maybe you just need a hobby, Darren? How about watching *Star Trek* reruns?"

Darren glared coldly at her, irritated by her comment. For a brief moment, she was afraid of him. Muriel felt the fleeting urge to apologize, but quickly decided against it, and kept silent.

"You really ought to take this situation seriously. I realize you may be angry that my grandfather caused the death of your granduncle, but you never really knew Professor Aubrey."

"But still, he was family," she whispered, glaring back at him.

Josephine arrived with Darren's coffee.

"Miss Aubrey," he cleared his throat, "if any of this is true, it could be a dangerous situation for you. If these creatures are real, they could be still here, especially since they live so long—"

He continued on about the potential threat to human life and safety, talking quietly, almost in a whisper. But she noticed people in the diner were staring at Darren, and listening. She tuned him out long enough to think of something. She had to get the notes away from him. They were the evidence. "Darren? Have you ever shown that notebook to anyone else?"

"Not to anyone outside the family. It's all just too unbelievable."

"Yeah. That's good." She smiled at him, and suddenly pretended to be interested. "Well, if you want me to believe you, then can I borrow it and read it? I mean, you obviously know where I live."

He inhaled and hesitated. "Well, I suppose that would be okay. You must have a set of notes of your own, don't you? Your uncle must have kept volumes—"

She reached to take it from his hand. "Thanks, Darren. I promise this will be safe."

He suddenly gazed coldly at Muriel as he held onto the book more tightly, "You will return it, won't you?"

"Of course I will! I just need to read it. I mean, you want me to believe you, about vampires being in this town, about them being real and all that? How can I believe something like that, unless I see the evidence?"

"Okay, then." He exhaled slowly, and seemed to relax as he let it go, "As long as I can get it back when you're done reading through it."

They finished their coffee. He continued on about his being worried for her. He had a daughter her age. He knew she lived alone. The notes said they do drink blood; it was a fact. She should be careful not to go out at night. He couldn't be sure if they still were in the area...

She told him it was late. She had studying to do. And she was tired.

"Is there something you're not telling me, Miss Aubrey?"

"No." She wondered if he knew she was lying.

She drifted out into the ice-covered parking lot, alone. She really was tired. And she was worried about Darren's sanity and everyone else's safety. She thought about the tremendous losses the vampires had suffered throughout the centuries, and felt that they deserved better. She herself was orphaned while a young child and knew how it felt to lose family.

"Good job," it was Josie, following her out, quickly wrapping her leather bomber jacket around herself. "You got it. You got that stupid sixth book. And an Academy Award for best actress."

The notebook was tucked under Muriel's coat. "Yeah. So what the hell are we gonna do now? You heard that guy. He thinks . . . "

"We know what he thinks." It was Karl coming toward her, followed by Sophie. They had been in the diner, pretending to enjoy coffee they didn't actually touch. "We need to get worried. But we can't do anything. Not just yet. We don't want him to get scared. He'll start yapping his mouth off if he does, or worse. Then we'll get tabloid reporters running around town when they run low on Bigfoot stories and UFO crap."

"Yeah. Probably get a bunch of wanna-be Goth kids floating around town too." She yawned and reached for her car keys. "Want it?" she held out the notebook.

Sophie took it, read a few pages in near total darkness. "Here," she handed it back. "You've kept the others safe enough. Hide it with the rest of them. We've all got some thinking to do."

The wind howled and it began to snow, flurries blew about the parking lot. Muriel said she hoped the roads wouldn't be bad going back to school in the morning.

"Yes," said Sophie. "We don't need another terrible storm."

"He'll be back for it, you know."

"We know, Muriel," Sophie said. "We know."

"Sophie? What are we gonna do?"

Sophie didn't answer. "Take care of yourself. Drive carefully."

After a long day at college and a long drive home, she spread her textbooks out on the table where she previously had her uncle's notes, realizing she'd rather be reading his dusty old papers than the boring subject she was trying to plow through now.

And a term paper was due next month, damn it. On what? She hadn't decided on what to do for her term paper, but it needed to be twenty pages long, at least, with thirty items or more listed for the bibliography, and students were strictly warned by the instructor not to use too many internet sources... *I know cut and paste when I see it. And some of you buy your papers online,* he said. *Believe me, I can tell which ones are real.*

And then she would be required to stand up before the class and give a presentation. She hated that. It dawned on her that she ought to buy a computer for home use, now that she could finally afford one. The computer room on campus was closed after hours, and the library in the small town only had five out-of-date computers for the public. She wondered if those were the only computers in the entire town.

And she wondered what her uncle would think of college life today. The classrooms weren't heated very well, and people sat all morning in their coats. Cell phones rang all during the lecture, and the girl who sat next to her started a conversation with her boyfriend while everyone else was trying to pay attention. *"But he's calling from Aruba!"*

Muriel thought it pretty juvenile when spitballs flew across the room. "Hey, this isn't first grade! This is college! Knock it off!" People in class, including the instructor, applauded when she turned and said that, and so tonight she felt good about herself. Yeah, she thought, and if you do it again, my friends will come and bite your dumb ass.

"So wow, you own a house?" She got that at least a couple of times in the cafeteria. "Is it like real run-down and stuff?"

"Nope. Not too bad. Pretty dusty, though. Had to clean it up real good. Almost everything works okay. The stuff in the kitchen is out of date, gotta buy a new refrigerator, new stove, fix a broken window and stuff. But it's livable. The neighbors are pretty okay." But she didn't mention about the neighbors being vampires, or her stalker the boring accountant, or what she found hidden behind the cleanout door. But she also surprised herself to suddenly be discussing home repair issues like a grown-up, instead of talking about what happened last night at some club and who got drunk. "I want to get new curtains too. And get some electrical things fixed. Maybe I'll even buy one of those books about how to fix stuff, and figure it out myself, just for the hell of it. "

She was glad to get back to see her friends Sheree, Akeem, and Lacey. Since she had moved into the old house the people she associated with were much older than her, even though they didn't look it—all except for Josie. And seeing her friends took her mind off Darren...

The barely functioning doorbell rang.

"Who the hell could that be?" She put the book down and looked out the window into the driveway and saw her car, and an SUV. She knew no one locally with such a massive truck. "Damn it. It must be him, looking for his stupid notebook." She really didn't want to speak to him right now. She killed the lights back in kitchen, pulled the curtains, and hoped he would just go away.

She was used to the dark by now anyway.

"Miss Aubrey? Are you all right in there?"

Oh shit. This guy thinks he's looking out for my welfare. If she answered the door he would demand to know why she turned the lights out, then demand his book back, and he'd probably follow her to where she kept it and try and get all the rest of the notes away from her...

"Miss Aubrey? Everything okay?"

She remained silent.

"Are you all alone?"

Oh God, what a freak this guy is.

There was a massive loud pounding on the door, then another.

"What the—" He was ramming his shoulder against the door, trying to break in. "He really is crazy—"

With a crash the door flew open. She screamed.

"*Leave me alone! I'll call the cops. Get the hell away from me—*" she dashed around the kitchen, looking through where the knives were kept.

But he kept coming.

"Muriel!"

"Get the hell outta my house!"

"But, Muriel—"

Finally she found a knife. "Get away from me or I'll—

"*Get the hell away from her, you crazy son of a bitch!*" A new voice broke into the darkness. She almost didn't recognize it through its rage.

"*Elton?*"

With the moonlight that drifted through the windows, she saw Darren thrown to the ground. He howled in sudden pain and fear. She switched on a light.

"Oh thank God, Elton—"

"I was driving to the store and saw this guy's truck. Then I heard you scream."

"Who's this?" Darren mumbled. "Your boyfriend?"

"Darren. Shut the hell up. This is the man who is rescuing me from you, you strange weirdo." She put the knife back. "What the hell made you break into my house? Are you crazy? You want your book back so bad you break into my house? What the hell were you trying to do? You scared the crap outta me. I almost thought you were gonna—"

"Tell this goon to let me go," he struggled against Elton's grip and Elton told him to be quiet.

"No, I won't. You just broke into my house. What the hell is wrong with you?"

Elton patted down Darren's jacket. "He's got no weapon. Just this cross." It fell out of Darren's pocket and onto the floor.

"I was worried about you. I knew you were home, you didn't answer the door. Then the lights went out. I was—*ouch!* Will you let me go?" But Elton only held tighter. "I thought something had happened to you."

The ice cold wind now blew throughout the already drafty home.

"What? You busted down my door so you could see if I was okay?"

"Idiots never change," said Elton. "What do you want me to do with this reject?" He pulled Darren up so he could stand but still gripped his arm.

"I hope you won't call the police?" Darren looked at her pleadingly. "This wouldn't look good when I go to apply for a job."

"You broke my door down, and now I'm gonna freeze my ass off all night and catch pneumonia because of you! And all you can think of is applying for a job."

"I'll pay for the damage. I have got enough saved for minor expenses. Look, Muriel. This is a big misunderstanding. I'm very sorry. Now will this guy let me go?"

Elton released him. "Fine. But don't try anything stupid. You've got some explaining to do."

"I was just worried about her. The lights went out, and she didn't answer."

"Like maybe I was studying, so I got tired?" She stood there, shivering. She noticed Darren was shivering now despite his heavy parka. Elton only wore a thin leather jacket but didn't seem to mind the cold as much. Flurries now blew into the hallway.

"That was really stupid, you know," Elton said to Darren. "Muriel, we should call the police."

Muriel reached for the phone on the wall. Darren rushed to try and leave through the door he busted down, but Elton caught him and threw him back down on the ground like a rag doll. "You are going nowhere."

Then she noticed the look in Darren's eyes when he gazed up at Elton. Damn it. He knew it now. Somehow he just figured it out. Maybe because Elton was unusually strong and quick, or because his face was nearly as pale as moonlight. Somehow he just figured it all out.

"Wait a minute. Muriel," Elton said quietly. "Put the phone down."

"What? Don't you want me to call the cops?"

"Not yet. I think maybe we should just deal with this."

Darren continued to stare up at Elton from where he sat, finally motionless.

"Call Sophie first, and then call Karl." He turned back to Darren while Muriel dialed the old rotary phone. "Now look, why don't you just get yourself up off the floor and — "

"Why? Aren't you just going to tear me to shreds anyway?"

"*Now you just listen — *"

"Or are you waiting for friends to arrive so you can all share?"

Muriel turned while waiting for Sophie to pick up. "Darren! You just don't know what you're talking about. You are condemning some very decent people! Hello? Sophie... ? Uhm... like... We got a problem – "

Elton took over the conversation with Darren. "Now look, get off the damn floor," and he took his arm and hauled him up once again. "No one is going to tear you to shreds. And we don't like junk food, so go over there and sit yourself down." He led Darren through the kitchen into the living room. "You have a hell of a lot of explaining to do. And you're going to start now!"

"Sophie is coming over, and she'll get Karl." Muriel said, glad that Elton had the situation under control. "And I'm freezing!" She went to try and get the door to close properly. It wouldn't, so she pushed a chair up against it to block out the wind.

"Why should I explain anything? This situation is obvious," she heard Darren say. "I've figured out what you are, and now you're calling others – "

"I already said we won't kill you. What more do you want? A written contract? Start talking and stop whining. Why did you even come to this town in the first place?"

"I wanted to know the answers, once and for all. I just needed to know. "

Muriel explained to Elton what Darren had told her earlier about the sixth notebook. "He's kept it all this time, and couldn't stop wondering all his life about it. That's why he came here, finally. To know."

"I heard about that from Sophie—"

Muriel continued, "But what you don't know is that the sixth book just seems to focus on blood drinking, how much, how often, killing animals, drinking from an occasional person, stuff like that. There are a lot of empty pages, it's unfinished, and there's not much else. Darren, look," she said. "What you read is only a very small part of the whole story. You're just passing judgment without really knowing enough."

"And how the hell do you fit with all this, Miss Aubrey?" he demanded, still in fear for his life. "You know all about these... these creatures? Is this some Aubrey family tradition? Being friends to vampires?" He spat the words out in disgust.

"And you say that like it's a bad thing," Elton shot back. "Listen, idiot. Let's talk about your family history. Your grandfather not only killed her uncle, he killed my parents and my unborn brother or sister. I'll never know which. So is that why you've come back? To finish off the rest of us? What the hell took you so long? We were all doing fine until you came to town!"

Muriel had never seen Elton angry before. He had never been anything but quiet up until he met Darren.

"Yeah," she stammered out. "And were you gonna kill me, too?"

Darren sat staring at the both of them, speechless, until he finally got the words out. "Well... I had no idea he killed all those people. I always thought he and the professor got into some kind of argument over the notebook. No one in the family ever talked much about it."

"Well, we're talking now, Darren. Were you breaking into my place to kill me? Because saying you're busting in to protect me sounds like a pretty dumb excuse."

"He's not going to kill anyone now, Muriel. We've caught this bastard in time."

He looked back at Elton. "You really think I came all the way here to kill you all? And her?"

"*What else?*" Elton snarled.

"I've told you already. To learn the truth. Why can't you believe that?"

"And why can't you believe these people aren't all evil monsters?" she said.

"So it is true, then? They really do live off blood?" Darren shivered even more now, and looked paler than Elton.

"They don't need human blood, Darren," she tried to keep the rage out of her voice. "Can't you figure that out? They use animals. And no one has ever been hurt around this town, except them."

"Someone's at the door, Muriel," Elton said.

"Huh? I don't hear any—" But she went to answer it, pulling the chair aside so she could open the door. It was Sophie, with Karl in uniform. Behind them both was Seymour. "Hi guys," she said nervously.

"I see what our guest has done with the door," said Seymour.

"Yup. Breaking and entering," Karl said with a grim smile.

Sophia brushed a hand across her frozen cheek as they all stood in the doorway. "Were you harmed, child?"

"N-no. I got pretty scared, though, when he came charging in like that. Elton heard the noise and came in after him. He's got him in the living room. He tried to get away, too. But Elton caught him and dragged him back in."

They came in and Karl helped put the door back together again to block out the wind. On the way to the living room she could hear Elton repeating once again, "No. We will definitely not kill you. Okay? I thought I already cleared that up?"

Darren then looked up at the three of them, not even noticing Muriel. But she saw the look of frozen terror in his eyes when he saw them walk in. He tried to speak, but his throat was dry and his voice broke up. Muriel could see that he was shaking.

Seymour leaned against the wall and glared at him. Elton stayed where he was, sitting directly in front of him, making sure he couldn't leave. Sophie took the couch with Karl, who then leaned forward and started. "You know. I could bring you in for breaking and entering, assault, stalking... hell, I can write a big long list. Was that your vehicle in a handicapped space the other night — "

He stopped speaking suddenly, then Sophie looked at the ceiling and let out a sigh. Seymour stood motionless, and Elton seemed to cringe slightly... then finally, Muriel noticed the smell. And she saw Darren's worn out jeans were soaked through. He had soiled himself. A stifled sob escaped his throat.

"Oh..." She felt bad for him, but it was all she could say.

"Fearless vampire hunter," Seymour hissed, slightly baring his teeth.

"Seymour." Elton didn't move, despite the stench. "Knock it off."

"Wanna clean up?" Muriel asked from where she stood. "Do you have extra clothes in your truck? I know you've been like wandering around and — "

Darren didn't answer.

"Look, Darren," Elton went on, more quietly this time. "I'm saying it again. No one will hurt you. We just want to figure out what your plans are. Why you've come here. What you want. And what you're going to do about discovering us. That's all we want. We don't want to frighten you or hurt you."

He said something incoherent and then he finally stammered out, "Nothing! I won't do anything about anything. I only wanted to know, that's all. That's the truth. *I'm not here to cause any trouble — "*

"But why did you break into my house?" demanded Muriel. She sat down between Sophie and Karl. "I mean, you scared the crap outta me."

"I thought... I thought you were in danger. The lights went out. You wouldn't answer. I thought something was happening to you—"

"I didn't want to answer the door, okay? I just didn't feel like talking to you. And why would anything happen in this quiet little nothing town?"

"Well, knowing your family history, I thought—"

"What? My uncle wasn't murdered by someone like them," there was rage in her voice now. "He was murdered by someone like you!"

"But he gave himself to—" he couldn't finish. "I thought that it was happening to you, too."

"*Huh?*"

"I'll tell you later, dear," Sophie put a hand on her shoulder.

"*Is there something else I don't know about my uncle... ?*"

"Mr. Michelson," Sophie began. "Ben was a grown man, able to make his own decisions about who he loved. Your grandfather came to this town because he was against mixing races. He killed a man and his wife and their unborn child. And he killed Ben when he got in the way. And he would have killed me as well if he knew where to find me then. And thank God for justice because he got what he deserved. And we want to know why you've come, because all we want is to just live. Is that too much to ask?"

Darren was silent. The wind howled outside, and Muriel felt the draft from the broken door.

"I... I didn't know," he started again. "I thought the Professor had been under some sort of influence. And when the lights went out, I was worried and —"

They talked on through the night. Darren's pants seemed to dry up but the smell still lingered in the room. Muriel hoped the draft from the broken door would air the house out. She went to get her heavy sweater to keep warm, then brewed herself and Darren coffee. She was relieved that he finally seemed to calm down somewhat. Around midnight, Seymour went to the cheap motel where Darren had been staying to pick up his duffel bag with his spare set of clothes.

She heard Elton say it can take a person anywhere from a few minutes to a few years to stop being afraid when they first find out. The difference, he believed, was not just knowing that vampires were not really out to randomly kill people, but in realizing that they were just people like everyone else. People who needed to keep a secret. People whose very lives could be in danger if anyone found out.

Finally toward dawn he agreed not to say a word to anyone and to leave the sixth notebook with them. He promised once again to pay for repairing the front door, and Muriel promised to not press charges. Before he finally left, she found a plastic trash bag for his pants. He used her downstairs bathroom to clean up and change.

Two weeks later Josie and Muriel went to visit Annasophia again. Muriel brought with her all six notebooks. When they arrived they saw she had been repairing the old sable coat by hand, putting in a new silk lining, and also making a dress to sell in her shop. The fire was blazing, keeping the room warm.

Muriel also brought with her a letter that arrived in the mail along with a check covering the damages. She read it outloud. In it, Darren expressed his apologies to everyone, especially Muriel.

Sophie sat and laughed quietly as she listened.

"Why don't we just burn them, Sophie?" Muriel said. "Just get rid of them all?"

"No! Don't. I couldn't let you do that. After all that work Ben did with us. It would be wrong. So very wrong. Don't. No. I have a better idea, which is why I've called you to come over. It's not to sit and watch me stitch, girls. Stay there," she got up to leave the room. "And don't do anything to those books."

She came back with a steel box with a combination lock. "I bought this last week. It's time to put them all away somewhere really safe." She opened it, and Muriel put the books in. The lid was locked tight.

"Just one thing I don't understand, Sophie," Josie asked, "is why you left them at the Professor's house that night? Why didn't you take them home with you and hide them somewhere better?"

"Well... this is where it gets complicated. Back then, people knew Ben and I were seeing each other. Ben was killed at the home of Elton's parents, you may recall. He met Darren's grandfather there, and he tried to prevent the tragedy, but he was too late to help. I raised Elton after his parents were killed. That house was sold, and the money was put into trust for Elton. He bought another house, where he still is now.

"As soon as I found out, I went into a terrible state of disbelief. Seymour came to me and told me the night after your granduncle was killed. I went cold, and refused to believe, until he showed me the paper. He tore the story out, and handed it to me. 'Look, see, I told you.' I ran through the fields to Ben's house. Back then, people didn't always lock their doors, especially in small towns. I went in, called out for him, shouted out his name in hysteria. I just didn't want to believe it. I heard a car come, and looked out the window. It was the police, probably coming to search the place. I grabbed the notes off his desk, and they were coming through the front door, which I had left open. I ran into the basement to hide, and quickly shoved the notebooks into the place where you would find them so many years later. And I believe you were meant to find them. His spirit guided you, perhaps. It's how I know he somehow lives on. I was in a panic that night. I didn't want to be caught with them. I knew the police might probably come to my house later to find his research, which that murdering bastard continued to rave on about before they finally pulled the switch... I ran out the door that leads out of the basement, went back home through the woods so I wouldn't be seen. To this day, I don't believe the police knew I had been in the house. I really did want to go back to get them, but somehow I couldn't. Too many memories, too much sadness. And so much guilt over his death. I still wonder if it was my fault.

"You see, his trusted colleague not only found out about the research when Ben foolishly went to him to discuss it, and found out about Elton's parents, a mixed marriage as you know — but Ben had been bringing me to social functions at the University. He figured out about us. I was a foreign woman, from a small town, but had much jewelry from the old country, and I could make dresses more beautiful than those worn by Hollywood stars. I felt I could fit in with his sophisticated friends. He did not tell anyone our secret, except that we were planning to marry. That was no secret. Yes, Muriel, dear child, we were planning to have a life together. I didn't intend for it to be that way when I first met him. But as time went on, somehow, it just happened.

"We fell in love. He looked older than me, but I was actually older than he was. It didn't matter. But how did the secret get out then? I'll tell you. And that was my fault. We were driving around in his car one night, just driving for no reason, as people did then. Gas was cheap, and cars were big and comfortable. People just drove for enjoyment. We stopped by the lake to watch the moon in the sky. It was a beautiful night. The lake was all silver, the sky was black velvet. Yes, something happened, Muriel. The next morning he went back to the University, harmless little scar on his neck. It was not long after that when the trouble started —" She looked away, not able to face them. "I never told the others where I put them. Seymour wanted to burn all his papers, or toss them in the lake. I just couldn't. The notes were all that was left of Ben. I thought of going back into the old house to get them. But I just somehow couldn't even look at them ever again… Until you found them."

"I never knew that about my uncle. If things had been different, we would have been sort of related, Sophie."

"It was terrible for all of us. We had all left the old country a century earlier after a terrible massacre. Ten of us butchered in our homes while we slept. We came to America to find peace. See?" and she held out her delicate white hand. "He gave me this. I never took it off." A ruby surrounded by diamonds. Muriel had always admired the ring, but never asked about it. "I am still to this day broken-hearted," Sophie went on. "In all the time I've lived, Ben was the only man I've ever really loved." A tear rolled down her cheek. She wiped it away.

"You so much remind me of him. If ever we had a daughter, she'd be like you." She handed Muriel the steel box. "Someday, maybe the world will be ready to see them, and then to know the truth. But for now, hide them well."

More Books from Bathory Gate Press

Beyond the Count, ed. Margo Bond Collins

Long before Dracula, vampires stalked the literary scene.

These early literary vampires are sometimes terrifying, at times melodramatic, and occasionally ridiculous, but they are always out for blood — and their vampiric descendants continue to fascinate and captivate us.

Beyond the Count includes an edited collection of vampire stories, plays, and poems from the eighteenth and nineteenth centuries, annotated and introduced by literary scholar Margo Bond Collins. This collection gives students, scholars, and vampire aficionados alike the opportunity to examine works often long out of print and to contextualize the development of the vampire beyond that most famous of literary Counts.

Never Upon a Time by Meredith Jade

You've always hated her, but you might not know the whole story. . .

Edith may not be brazen and enchanted like her twin sister, Ember, but in a world of dying magic, perhaps her simple desires are enough.

After a Selection Banquet gone awry, Edith is left without a suitor or a plan. Befriending a little white fox and occupying herself with a philanthropic project outside castle walls, Edith soon rebuilds morale and musters enough courage to reach out to her estranged twin sister.

But Ember's been harboring an evil secret - and thwarted love and jealous can turn acts of merit into classic tales of wickedness in this new twist on an old tale.

Sanguinary, **A Night Shift Novel by Margo Bond Collins**

Sometimes the monsters in the dark are real.

As a child, Lili Banta ignored her grandmother's cryptic warnings to avoid children outside their Filipino community in Houston. When many of those other children fell ill, Lili ignored the whispers in her community that a vampiric *aswang* walked among them.

Years later, Lili returns to Houston to work for the Quarantine Station of the Center for Disease Control—but she is plagued by dark, bloody dreams that consume her nights and haunt her days. When a strange illness attacks the city's children, Lili is called in to find its source, and maybe even a cure.

But in order to save the city, she must first acknowledge the sinister truth: A monster stalks the night—closer than she ever expected....

Bound by Blood, A Night Shift Novella
by Margo Bond Collins

Only fifty years left before vampires rule the world.

When Dallas police detective Cami Davis joined the city's
vampire unit, she planned to use the job as a stepping-stone to a
better position in the department.

But she didn't know then what she knows now: there's a silent
war raging between humans and vampires, and the vampires are
winning.

So with the help of a disaffected vampire and an ex-cop addict,
Cami is going undercover, determined to solve a series of recent
murders, discover a way to overthrow the local Sanguinary
government, and, in the process, help win the war for the human
race.

But can she maintain her own humanity in the process? Or will
Cami find herself, along with the rest of the world, pulled under a
darkness she cannot oppose?

Made in the USA
Middletown, DE
09 September 2015